Mrs. Greenberg's Messy Hanukkah

Linda Glaser   Illustrated by Nancy Cote

SCHOLASTIC INC.

New York   Toronto   London   Auckland   Sydney
Mexico City   New Delhi   Hong Kong   Buenos Aires

To Helen, who opens her home and her heart to countless friends, and who opened the way for this book. Thank you.—L.G.

To Mike—your tireless energy, compassion, and love are a gift to all, but a treasure to me.—N.C.

ISBN-13: 978-0-545-11560-5
ISBN-10: 0-545-11560-4

Text copyright © 2004 by Linda Glaser. Illustrations copyright © 2004 by Nancy Cote. All rights reserved. Published by Scholastic Inc., 557 Broadway, New York, NY 10012, by arrangement with Albert Whitman & Company. SCHOLASTIC and associated logos are trademarks and/or registered trademarks of Scholastic Inc.

12 11 10 9 8 7 6 5 4 3 2 1   8 9 10 11 12 13/0

Printed in the U.S.A.   40

First Scholastic printing, September 2008
The design is by Carol Gildar.

Potato Latkes (for 4 or 5 people)

6 medium-sized potatoes
1 egg
1 small onion
3 T. flour, matzo meal, or bread crumbs
1 tsp. salt
oil—enough to almost cover latkes in frying pan

Rachel helps–Scrub and peel potatoes. Grate potatoes and onion.
Pour off extra liquid. Add egg, flour, and salt. Mix.
Mama helps–Drop potato mixture into hot oil with tablespoon.
Fry both sides until golden brown. Drain on clean towel.
Rachel helps–Clean up the mess.
Mrs. Greenberg helps–Serve hot with applesauce or sour cream.

Enjoy with friends!

"*Please* can we make potato latkes today?" Rachel sat at the kitchen table swinging her legs. "And let's invite Mrs. Greenberg for dinner!"

"Enough with the latkes!" Mama threw her hands in the air. "I told you already, we'll make them next week when the relatives come. *That's* when we'll invite Mrs. Greenberg."

"But tonight won't even feel like the first night of Hanukkah." Rachel took the menorah from the cupboard and pushed the first two candles in. "No latkes. No company."

"We'll still light the candles." Mama kissed her on the nose. "It'll be Hanukkah. Don't worry. But right now, Papa and I have lots of errands. So please get your coat on."

Rachel set the menorah on the windowsill. It was such a cold, gray day out there, just the kind that begged you to make the house all warm and good-smelling. That gave her an idea.

"Can I stay next door with Mrs. Greenberg?"

"All afternoon?" Mama shook her head.

"Please?" asked Rachel.

"She's not so used to little monkeys."
Papa gave Rachel a playful poke.

"But it's almost Hanukkah. And she's
all alone," Rachel pointed out. "She could
use a little company."

"Hmm. I didn't think of that. Well, I
suppose . . ." Mama looked at Papa. "If you
won't be any trouble . . ."

"I'm never any trouble!" Rachel pulled
on her coat and raced out the door,
braids flying.

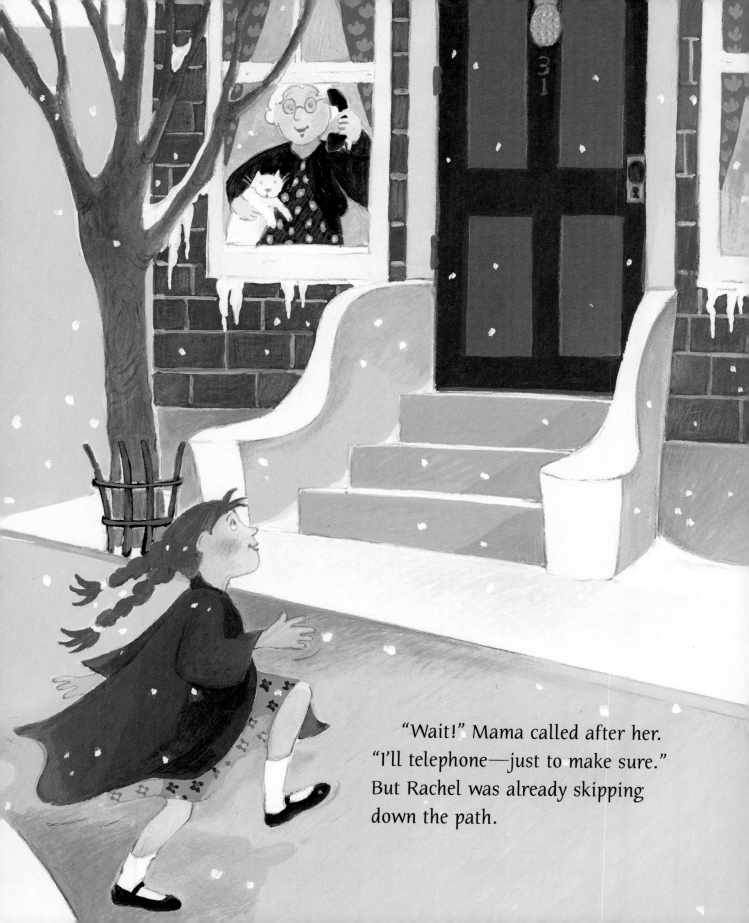

"Wait!" Mama called after her.
"I'll telephone—just to make sure."
But Rachel was already skipping
down the path.

Mrs. Greenberg's house was all clean and sparkly like it was just *waiting* for company, while Rachel's house always looked like it was still in bed with its hair sticking up. And Mrs. Greenberg was always glad to see her.

"Come in! Don't be a stranger," said Mrs. Greenberg. "I told your dear mama of course you can stay. It's much too empty around here—especially for Hanukkah."

Rachel stepped inside. "That's just what I told her." She peeled off her coat. "Can we make latkes?"

"Oh, my," said Mrs. Greenberg. "I haven't made latkes in years."

"But latkes make it feel like Hanukkah," Rachel explained.

"It's *some* messy job," said Mrs. Greenberg. "All that grating and frying."

"But Mama and Papa would be so surprised!" Rachel jumped in the air.

"Hmm. I didn't think of that. I *do* have plenty of potatoes."

"Wonderful!" Rachel exclaimed. She skipped into the kitchen where everything had its very own place and it all sparkled, even the floor.

Mrs. Greenberg handed her an apron and they both got right to work grating potatoes. Rachel tried to keep her gratings in a nice little hill like Mrs. Greenberg's. But somehow her little hill slid right off the table.

"Oops!" said Rachel.

"Oy!" said Mrs. Greenberg.

What a mushy mess! Rachel grabbed the mop. But the more she mopped, the worse it got.

"That's OK." Mrs. Greenberg took the mop. "I'll finish later. Don't you worry. After all, what's a little grated potato between friends?"

Next it was time for the egg. Rachel tried to crack it into the bowl just like Mama always did. But somehow it popped right out of her hands.

"Oops!" said Rachel.

"Oy!" said Mrs. Greenberg.

What a slippery mess! Rachel grabbed the mop. But the more she mopped, the worse it got.

"That's fine. I'll finish later." Mrs. Greenberg stepped over the shiny yellow streaks. "Don't you worry. After all, what's a little egg between friends?"
She gave a sigh.

"Soon we'll have Hanukkah latkes!" Rachel reminded her.

Mrs. Greenberg stirred everything in a big bowl.

Rachel lugged over a bag of flour. "Don't we need this?"

But somehow, the bag ripped. "Oops!" said Rachel.

"Oy!" said Mrs. Greenberg.

What a powdery mess! Rachel grabbed the mop. But the more she mopped, the worse it got.

"Never mind. I'll get it later," said Mrs. Greenberg. "Don't you worry. After all, what's a little flour between friends?" But she looked awfully tired.

"Soon it'll feel like Hanukkah!" Rachel reminded her. And she sure hoped it would!

At last, it was time to fry the latkes. Mrs. Greenberg checked the clock. "Your Mama and Papa will be here any minute. Quick, Rachel, drizzle a little oil into the pan."

"Mama uses *lots* of oil," said Rachel. "For the miracle of when the oil lasted eight days." But somehow, the oil came spurting out faster than Rachel had expected—much faster. "Oops!"

What a soppy mess! Rachel reached for the mop.

"Don't even bother." Mrs Greenberg sank into a chair in the living room.

"Just let me rest a few minutes. Anyway, what's a little oil after all this?" She flung her arm at the kitchen.

Rachel waited for the part about friends. But not a word. And nothing about "Don't you worry" either. Uh-oh! The kitchen was such a mess—like it might faint if it looked at itself in the mirror. What would Mama and Papa say?

Just then, the back door opened. "Anybody home?" called Papa.

Mama stepped into the kitchen. "Oh, no!"

"Surprise!" squeaked Rachel, trying to smile. "We're making latkes."

Mama and Papa did look surprised, but not the way Rachel had hoped. Not at all.

Papa pointed at the floor. "What's all this?!"

Mama frowned. "Rachel, look what you've *done.*"

Rachel's chin trembled. "I wanted to make it feel like Hanukkah.

But I made a terrible mess." A tear slid down her nose. "I'm sorry."

Mrs. Greenberg hurried over.

"Oh, *katchkeleh*, you dear little duck!" She rubbed the tear away with her thumb. "Actually, it's not a terrible mess. It's a *wonderful* mess. My house hasn't felt this lived-in in years."

"Really?" Rachel brightened up. "Well! I can make it lived-in anytime you want!"

Mrs. Greenberg laughed out loud. "Oh, darling, I'm sure you can!"

Rachel grabbed the mop. "Now let's *really* clean up!"
"Don't be silly. I'll do it later," said Mrs. Greenberg.
"Do me a favor," said Papa. "Sit down and relax."
"That's right," said Rachel. "*We* want to do it."

Mama tied on an apron and fried up the latkes crispy and hot, while Rachel and Papa cleaned up. Now the house was all sparkly, warm, and good-smelling.

Mrs. Greenberg lit the candles and said the blessings.

Finally everything was just how Rachel had imagined. "Thank you, Mrs. Greenberg." She beamed.

"Don't thank *me*. Thank *you*." Mrs. Greenberg grandly set
the latkes on the table. "*I've* got latkes *and* company."

"You sure do!" Rachel hugged Mrs. Greenberg
around her nice soft middle and gave a happy sigh.
"Now *this* feels like Hanukkah!"